G-BUGS
THE GRATITUDE BUGS™

In Front of The Class

Suite 300 - 990 Fort St
Victoria, BC, Canada, V8V 3K2
www.friesenpress.com

Text and illustrations copyright © 2015 by G.Bugs Press
First Edition — 2015

Library and Archives Canada Cataloguing in Publication
Jones, Jackie, 1953-
In Front of The Class / written and created by Jackie Jones ;
illustrated by George Athanasiou ; edited by Mike Muxlow.

(G-Bugs, the gratitude bugs)
ISBN
978-1-4602-6425-6 (Paperback)
978-1-4602-6426-3 (eBook)

I. Athanasiou, George, 1965- II. Title.
III. Series. Jones, Jackie, 1953- . G-Bugs, the gratitude bugs

PS8619.O5326F57 2011   jC813'.6   C2011-903679-7

1. Juvenile Fiction, Social Issues, Self-Esteem & Self-Reliance

Distributed to the trade by The Ingram Book Company

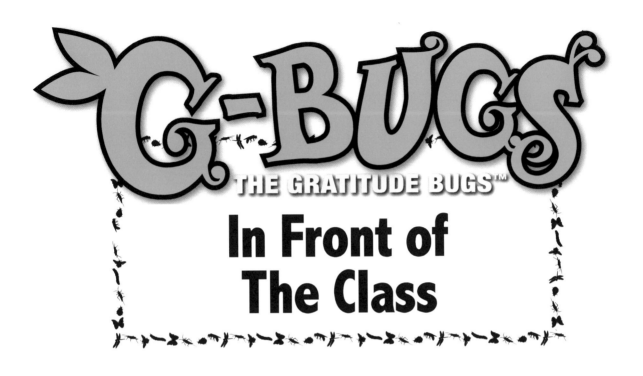

G-BUGS
THE GRATITUDE BUGS™

In Front of
The Class

Written and Created by **Jackie Jones**

Illustrated by **George Athanasiou**
Edited by **Mike Muxlow**

**ACCEPTANCE GRATEFULNESS SELF-ESTEEM HONESTY INTEGRITY
RESPONSIBILITY RESPECT FORGIVENESS LOYALTY FRIENDSHIP**

To Miss Clark and teachers everywhere,

It is truly wonderful that students have at least one teacher in their lifetime that is a great influence on his or her personality, growth and development.

Academically and socially, teachers find ways to enhance their students' wellbeing in both the present and the future.

Thank you teachers everywhere for being remarkable gifts.

Gratefully,
The G-Bugs Team

Foreword

I think by reading this book, children and "grown ups" will learn to understand that being different is ok and to not be upset about being themselves.

Over the past years of going to my local Public School teachers have told me and many other children that being different is truly one of the best parts of being you.

Caterpillar Kaleb, Bumble.B.Riley, Firefly Travis and Butterfly Rebecca are all great examples of just how important being different is, to not just the reader but to the people around them as well.

The Gratitude Bugs have helped me realize that every person is unique and has their own personality and story. If someone is different you shouldn't tell them to be more like you, you should celebrate their differences. Don't change who you are, because you are perfect just the way you are.

A fellow pupil told me once that I was kooky and different and that I should change to be like everyone else. But I think that being myself is really important. If I was like everyone else I wouldn't be *ME*. My parents encourage me to be an individual and I appreciate that.

I think that all of The Gratitude Bugs books show that being different is one of the most interesting things about you, and that we should be grateful about being ourselves. We also have many other reasons to be thankful too!

I always enjoy reading Jackie's books and I hope you do too.

Maggie R. – Gannaw, Age 10
Simcoe County Public School Student

Miss Emma cleared her throat, "Ah-hem. Now children, it's time for our weekly show and share. Sam, you may begin and we will listen carefully," she announced.

Sam had butterflies in his tummy as he went to a box and took out some small containers.

Caterpillar Kaleb was curled up in the first jar that Sam put on Dante's desk.

"This is Caterpillar Kaleb! I found him in my garden and he limps when he walks."

The children gathered closer. Some were on their tippy toes and others were practically climbing on top of Dante to get a better look.

"Caterpillar Kaleb is proud of who he is. He likes that he is different and it made me realize that people are different too. I call him my Gratitude Bug because I am grateful I met him," Sam stated.

"That is a very good lesson Sam," said Miss Emma. "And what special creature are you sharing with us next?"

There were 'oohs' and 'ahhs' as the children went to Ellie's desk where Sam placed the next container. Bumble B. Riley was buzzing happily in his jar.

Some of the students stood towards the back because they were afraid they might get stung.

"This is Bumble B. Riley and don't worry, he won't sting you." Sam explained.

The children sighed with relief.

"Bumble B. Riley wears glasses," Sam said. The class giggled with surprise!

"Wait!" said Sam. "We all know someone who wears glasses."

Alex spoke up and said, "Yes, but she's not a bug!"

The students laughed out loud. Miss Emma raised her hand and everyone went silent.

"Do you have a question, Miss Emma?" Sam asked.

"Yes. Why does a bumblebee need reading glasses like I do?"

Sam replied, "Bumble B. Riley has a little brother with Autism. His name is Henry B. and sometimes he flies away from the hive and can't remember how to get back home."

"Before glasses, Bumble B. Riley couldn't help look for his brother, but now, he can lead the search party!" Sam explained.

"Bumble B. Riley is grateful he can see so he is a Gratitude Bug too!" said Sam.

Clapping her hands, Miss Emma said, "That is another good lesson. Can you tell us about your pretty butterfly?" she asked.

Sam walked over to Harry's desk and held up Butterfly Rebecca for everyone to see.

"Does anyone here have a beauty mark like Butterfly Rebecca?" Sam asked.

"I have one!" Ellie shouted, as she rolled up her sleeve and pointed to her elbow. "My mom calls it a birthmark and says that each one is different."

"And now for my final surprise. This is Firefly Travis!" Sam announced as he took the large glass jar from Miss Emma's desk and held it high in the air.

There was Firefly Travis peeking out from under the grass.

"Is it okay if we turn off the lights, Miss Emma?" Sam asked.

Miss Emma smiled and calmly asked the children to be quiet as she reached for the light switch… and then… the room went dark.

Sam could feel his heart pounding as he wished and hoped that his idea would work.

He knew Firefly Travis was not very confident and usually pretty negative.

Sam whispered to Firefly Travis, "You can do this Firefly Travis! I believe in you!"

A few moments passed. The children waited anxiously. Nothing happened.

Sam whispered encouragingly, "I believe in you, now YOU need to believe in YOU Firefly Travis."

The children began to cheer. "Come on Firefly Travis! You can do it! TRA-VIS, TRA-VIS, TRA-VIS!"

It started as a flicker then suddenly, a flash of light.

ZZZZZAAAPPPPP!!!

The whole room lit up with a bright yellow light! Firefly Travis was glowing!

The class and the Gratitude Bugs were jumping and cheering with happiness! Firefly Travis did not let them down. They believed in him and he believed in himself.

As Sam put the Gratitude Bugs safely back in the box, Miss Emma asked the class what they had learned from Sam's presentation.

"We should be grateful we have friends and that we are all different!" Campbell shouted.

"It feels good to help others!" offered Katherine.

Cali thought it was important not to bully somebody because they are different.

"I think we need to believe we can do anything!" George said.

"Thank you, those are all very good answers," commented Miss Emma. "I believe Sam and the Gratitude Bugs were meant to teach us that we have many reasons to be grateful."

The whole class gave Sam and the Gratitude Bugs a standing ovation!

Just then there was a knocking at the classroom window. Everyone looked over to see a colorful dragonfly tapping against the glass.

Just Like a Gratitude Bug

Be grateful for your difference,
Be happy who you are,
Be proud, help out, be positive,
You were born a Superstar!

Be grateful for the things you have,
While you learn in school each day,
Keep reading, growing, sharing, caring,
And pay it back some way.

You've got to love 'you' first,
Be kind, just give a hug,
Dream big, believe and think good thoughts,
Just like a Gratitude Bug!

About the Author

Jackie Jones (nee Lameront) was born in Kingston, Ontario and is the eldest of eight siblings. Being from a large family, Jackie is very familiar with the importance of responsibility, patience and acceptance. Now living in the Village of Thornton, Jackie and her husband, Henry, have five children and eight wonderful grandchildren.

Inspired by Napoleon Hill, Jackie combined her passion for writing with her love of children to create The Gratitude Bugs series. When she's not writing new adventures for G-Bugs, reading, taking walks or learning guitar, Jackie helps Henry run Roadshow Antiques North in Innisfil, a business they've owned since 1995 and more recently, the Roadshow Antiques South in Pickering.

Living her life by the Law of Attraction, Jackie enjoys sharing G-Bugs stories with students in the primary grades. Her belief is that discussing the traits and differences of each character will help children recognize and identify with their core values. Jackie whole-heartedly believes that reading and sharing the stories of The Gratitude Bugs will bring hope and happiness to all children, from all walks of life, all around the world.

To contact Jackie please send an e-mail to *jackie@g-bugs.com*

A portion of sales from this book goes directly to help sick and abused children around the world.

Get more gratitude bugs at *www.g-bugs.com*

CPSIA information can be obtained
at www.ICGtesting.com
Printed in the USA
LVIC06n0202090515
437688LV00004B/8

* 9 7 8 1 4 6 0 2 6 4 2 5 6 *